Here come the fans.

D0352283

Here come the six ducks.

Here come the six foxes.

The duck fans quack.

The fox fans sing.

The ref rings a bell. The match has begun!

The foxes and ducks kick the ball.

Rick Duck gets the ball in.

Max Fox gets the ball in.

The ducks get the ball.

Max Fox kicks Rick Duck!

The duck fans quack.

The ref rings his bell.

Rick Duck gets the ball in!

The duck fans quack and sing.

The ducks win the match.